Harriet's
Halloween
Candy

HARRIET'S HALLOWEEN CANDY

20th ANNIVERSARY EDITION!

NANCY CARLSON

Carolrhoda Books, Inc. / Minneapolis

For my sister, Tuden, because she taught me to draw, and for my brother, David, because he withstood so much teasing and still grew up to be a nice guy!

Text and illustrations copyright © 2002 by Nancy Carlson

Carolrhoda Books, Inc.
A division of Lerner Publishing Group
241 First Avenue North
Minneapolis, MN 55401 U.S.A.

Website address: www.lernerbooks.com

Library of Congress Cataloging-in-Publication Data

Carlson, Nancy.
    Harriet's Halloween candy / by Nancy Carlson — 20th Anniversary ed.
      p.   cm.
    Summary: Harriet learns the hard way that sharing her Halloween candy makes her feel much better than eating it all herself.
    ISBN: 0–87614–913–1 (lib. bdg. : alk. paper)
    [1. Halloween—Fiction. 2. Sharing—Fiction. 3. Candy—Fiction. 4. Dogs—Fiction.] I. Title.
PZ7.C21665 Har 2002
    [E]—dc21   2001007517

Manufactured in the United States of America
1 2 3 4 5 6 – JR – 07 06 05 04 03 02

Harriet really got a lot of candy on Halloween.

When she got home, she laid it all out carefully
on the floor. Then she organized it. First by color.
Then by size. And finally by favorites.

Harriet's little brother Walter watched.
He was too little to go trick-or-treating.

"Harriet, you be sure you share your candy
with Walt," said Harriet's mother.

"No!" said Harriet. "It's all mine."

But Harriet felt a little guilty.

"Oh, all right," she said. She reached
into her bag and pulled out a teensy-weensy
piece of coconut candy.

Harriet didn't like coconut anyway.

Before Harriet went to bed, she packed her candy
in a big box.

Then she hid the box in her closet.

The next morning she got up early
to eat some of her candy.

After she finished three caramel-chocolate bars,
she hid the rest behind her bookcase.

Throughout the day Harriet checked on her candy.

She counted it.

Then she hid it in a new place every time.

Pretty soon Harriet was running out of places
to hide it.

"There's only one thing to do," said Harriet.
"I'll have to eat it all up."

So she started to eat.
First chocolate bars with peanuts.

Then licorice whips. Then peanut-butter cups.

Then red, blue, green, and orange gumdrops.

"Burp," she said when she got to the saltwater taffy.
"I don't feel so good."

"Maybe it's time to share."

"Wouldn't you like a sugar doughnut, Walt?"

"How about some caramel apples?"

"I'm so proud of you, Harriet," said Mother.
"Sharing is a sign of a grown-up dog."

"Oh," said Harriet, "I was going to share
all the time."

"That's good, Harriet," said Mother.
"Now go wash up for dinner."